Big and Small

By Jack Challoner

Contents

RSVP
RAINTREE
STECK-VAUGHN
PUBLISHERS
The Steck-Vaughn Company

Austin, Texas

Published by Raintree Steck-Vaughn Publishers, an imprint of
Steck-Vaughn Company

Editors: Kim Merlino, Kathy DeVico
Project Manager: Lyda Guz
Electronic Production: Scott Melcer

Photo Credits: cover: Tony Stone Images: top Johnny Johnson;
NHPA: bottom Steven Dalton;
J. Allan Cash: pp. 13, 18, 27;
Eye Ubiquitous: p. 4 NASA; p. 14 S. Nishinaga;
Robert Harding Picture Library: p. 26 Westlight/Bill Ross;
Science Photo Library: p. 6 Charles Falco; p. 7 Peter Menzel;
p. 11 Philippe Plailly/Eurelios; p. 15 CNRI; p. 19 James King-Holmes;
p. 24 Biophoto Associates; p. 25 Adam Hart-Davis; p. 31 Philippe Plailly;
Tony Stone Images: p. 3 Jerry Kabalenko; p. 23 Kim Blaxland;
p. 29 Ken Whitmore;
Park Street: p. 12;
Zefa: p. 16, 17, 20, 21, 22, 30.

Library of Congress Cataloging-in-Publication Data

Challoner, Jack.
Big and small / by Jack Challoner.
p.   cm. — (Start-up science)
Includes index.
ISBN 0-8172-4319-4
1. Size perception — Juvenile literature.   [1. Size.]   I. Title.   II. Series:
Challoner, Jack. Start-up science.
BF299.S5C48 1997
153.7'52 — dc20
95-48340
CIP
AC

Printed in Spain
Bound in the United States
1 2 3 4 5 6 7 8 9 0 LB 99 98 97 96

Big and Small

This book will answer lots of questions that you may have about big things and small things. But it will also make you think for yourself.

Each time you turn a page, you will find an activity that you can do yourself at home or at school. You may need help from an adult.

Why are some things bigger than others? Living things grow bigger as they become older. What things can you think of that are big or small?

Big Things

The size of something is how big or small it is. Big things take up lots of space, and very big things are usually very heavy.

Did you know?

Some trucks have tires that are more than 10 feet (3 m) tall. Ordinary cars have tires that are about 1.5 feet (.5 m) tall.

Big planet

This is Jupiter, one of the **planets** that moves around the sun. Jupiter is much bigger than the Earth.

Big food

Tomatoes are usually small enough to fit into the palm of your hand. But sometimes a tomato can grow much bigger, like this one has.

Now try this

See for yourself how much bigger Jupiter is than the Earth.

You will need:
modeling clay, a ruler

1. Make a ball of modeling clay ¹/₄ inch (³/₄ cm) wide. This is a model of the Earth.

2. Now make a ball of modeling clay 2 ³/₄ inches (5 ¹/₂ cm) wide for Jupiter. Compare it to your model of the Earth.

Small Things

What do you know that is small? It is sometimes important for things to be small, so that they fit into a small space. A **model** is a small copy of a real thing.

Small computer

Did you know?

The first computers were very large. A computer that was as big as a room was needed to carry out simple tasks.

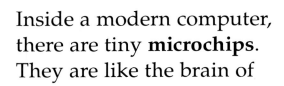

Inside a modern computer, there are tiny **microchips**. They are like the brain of the computer. This picture shows a microchip that is smaller than a fingernail.

Small model

This woman is making a very small model. She is using a magnifying lens to help her see because the model is so small. The magnifying lens makes her eye look very big.

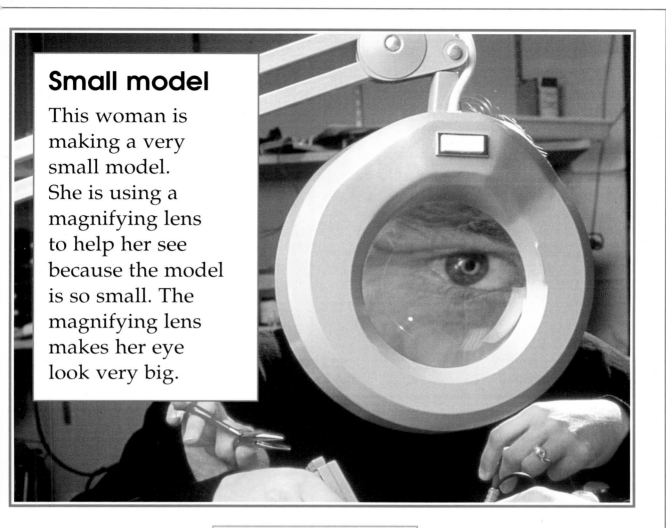

Now try this

A hand lens can make small things look bigger than they really are.

You will need:
a hand lens

1. Hold out the fingers of one hand.

2. Now hold the hand lens about 4 inches (10 cm) above your hand.

3. Look through the lens at your fingers. What do you notice?

Comparing Size

Some things are bigger than others. We can tell how big something is by putting other things next to it. This is called **comparing**.

Big shoes

These shoes are much too big for the boy's feet. They would fit a person with bigger feet. The boy needs smaller shoes.

Taller or shorter?

Compare the height of the girl in the middle with the heights of the boys. She is taller than the boy on the right. But she is shorter than the boy on the left.

Now try this

See if you can guess the size of your head.

You will need:
some string, a pair of scissors

1. Cut a piece of string to a length that you think will fit around your whole head.

2. Wrap another piece of string around your head. Ask a friend to cut this piece of string to the right length.

3. Compare the two pieces of string. How close was your guess?

Measuring Size

We usually use a tape measure or a ruler to measure the size of things. We use inches or centimeters to tell the size of an object.

Did you know?

The height of a horse is measured in hands. Hands are not all the same size, so people agree that one hand is about 4 inches (10 cm).

Measuring for fit

We sometimes need to be measured, to be sure that new clothes will be the right size. This man is using a tape measure to measure the boy's waist.

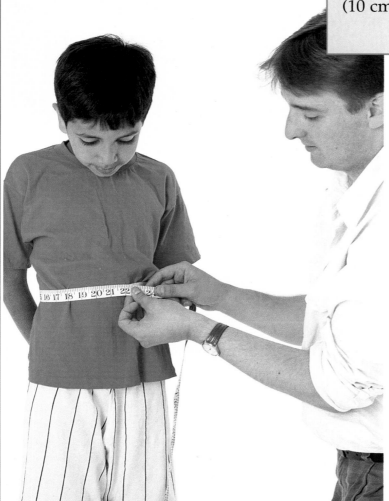

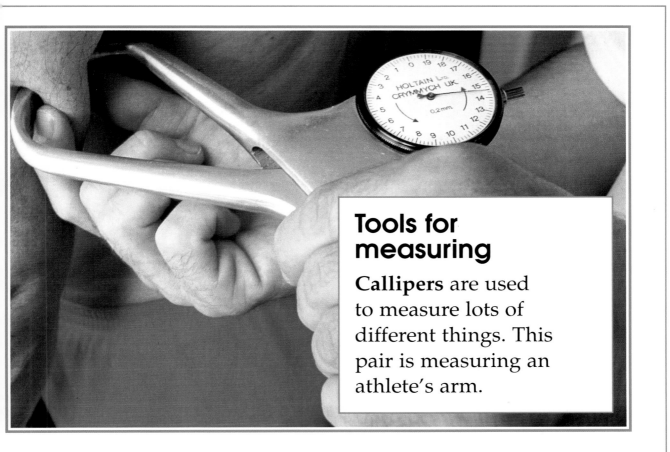

Tools for measuring

Callipers are used to measure lots of different things. This pair is measuring an athlete's arm.

Now try this

You can make your own set of callipers.

You will need:
cardboard, a paper fastener, a ruler

1. Cut two long, curved pieces of cardboard, both the same shape, as shown in the picture.

2. Ask an adult to help you join the two pieces together using the paper fastener.

3. Open your callipers, and close them around an object. Remove them without opening them.

4. Put the ends of the callipers onto the ruler, and read how wide apart they are.

Near or Far?

When things are close to us, they look bigger than when they are farther away. We can hardly see things that are really far away from us.

Did you know?

Stars are huge, but they are so far away that they appear as tiny points of light.

The same size?

This woman and the building look almost the same height. The building is really bigger, but it is much farther away.

Smaller and smaller

The people in this photograph seem to be smaller the farther away they are. The very farthest people appear as just dots.

Now try this

A coin is really much, much smaller than the moon, but it can look like it is the same size.

You will need:
a coin, a full moon

1. When there is a full moon outside, hold the coin in your hand, and hold your hand out.

2. Move your hand so that the coin covers the moon.

The moon is so far away that it seems to be the same size as the coin.

Under a Microscope

Some things are so small that you cannot see them by using just your eyes.

Looking at things through a **microscope** makes them look much bigger.

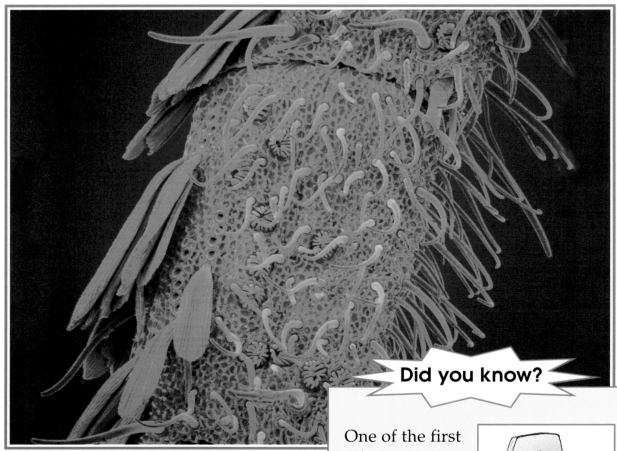

Close-up

This close-up picture shows one of a moth's antennae, which is very small. Under a microscope, you can see tiny hairs on the antennae.

Did you know?

One of the first microscopes that was ever made had a bead of glass in it. The bead looked like a drop of water.

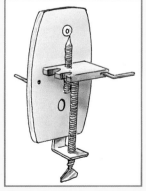

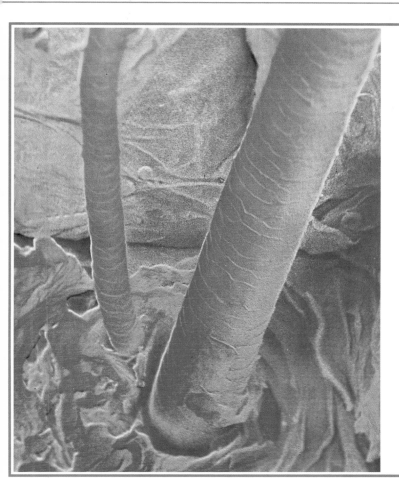

What is skin?

This is a picture of a person's skin that was taken through a microscope. The flat pieces are called skin **cells**, and the long pieces are hairs.

Now try this

You can make your own simple microscope. It will make some printed words look bigger.

You will need:
a magazine, water

1. Take a tiny drop of water on the end of your finger, and place it gently on some printed words.

2. Look at the printed words through the drop. They should look bigger than they really are.

Big Living Things

Animals that are very big are not often hunted by smaller animals. Their large size protects them. Big birds need large wings so that they can fly properly.

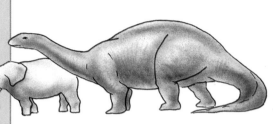

Huge hippo

This hippopotamus is about 10 feet (3 m) long. It is so big that only a few other animals can kill it.

Big bird

A heavy bird needs big wings to fly. Each wing of this albatross is nearly 6.5 feet (2 m) long.

Now try this

You can see for yourself how long the biggest hippos are.

You will need:
a long tape measure

1. Ask a friend to hold one end of the tape measure.

2. Now walk away from your friend, until there are 10 feet (3 m) between you. This is the size of a big hippo.

Small Living Things

Small living things can live without eating much food. But their small size means that they are in danger from bigger living things. Some are too small to even be seen.

Did you know?

Living things called **bacteria** are so small that you can only see them if you use a microscope.

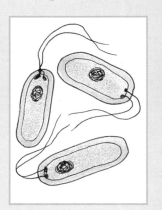

Small bird

The smallest bird in the world is the bee hummingbird.

It is only 2 inches (5 cm) long from head to tail.

Collecting insects

This man is using an **aspirator** to collect small insects. He can then study the insects before letting them go.

Now try this

You can make your own aspirator.

You will need:

an empty one-liter plastic bottle, two bendable straws, scissors, modeling clay

1. Cut 3 inches (8 cm) off the long end of one straw. Put both straws into the neck of the bottle.

2. Seal the straws with the bends above the bottle as shown using the modeling clay.

3. Hold the free end of the long straw over a small insect. Suck through the free end of the short straw. The insect will be sucked into the bottle.

4. Study the insect. Then put the insect back where you found it.

Growing Up

Most animals are born small and grow very quickly. They need food, which contains **nutrients**. Animals need nutrients in order to grow and to stay healthy.

Did you know?

The cuckoo lays its eggs in other birds' nests. The baby cuckoo grows faster than the other young birds in the nest.

Baby kangaroo

This kangaroo has a baby in her pouch. Inside the pouch, the young kangaroo sucks milk from a nipple. The milk contains nutrients.

Hungry birds

These young blackbirds receive nutrients from the food that their parents bring them. Soon they will grow to be as big as their parents.

Now try this

You can see for yourself how much young animals eat.

You will need:
a clean empty jar, aluminum foil, caterpillars and the leaves they are eating, a pencil

1. Place the caterpillars and the leaves you find them on in the jar.

2. Place the foil over the top of the jar. Make some small holes in it with the pencil.

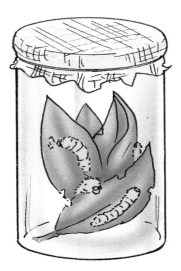

3. Look at the jar every day. Notice how much of the leaves are eaten.

4. After two days, return the caterpillars to where you found them.

Big Plants

Most plants grow bigger the longer they live. Some of the oldest plants are also the biggest. Many animals eat small plants, but big plants are often safe from animals.

Big trees

Giant redwood trees like this one are among the biggest trees in the world. The trunk of a redwood can be 360 feet (110 m) tall.

Did you know?

The leaves of arum trees, in Southeast Asia, are sometimes 10 feet (3 m) long.

Big flowers

The big colorful heads of these sunflowers attract many insects, such as bees.

Now try this

You can guess the size of a tree with the help of a friend.

You will need:
a tree, a friend

1. Ask a friend to stand in front of the tree.

2. Stand quite a long way away from the tree, and look at it. How many times would your friend fit into the height of the tree?

3. Ask your friend how tall he or she is. You can now figure out the

height of the tree. Ask an adult to help you.

Small Plants

Many small plants are not in danger because they are so small. Some plants are so tiny that they can only be seen through a microscope.

The smallest plants

Did you know?

Algae were some of the first living things on Earth. They live in oceans, ponds, and rivers. Algae often cover the surface of the water, making it look green.

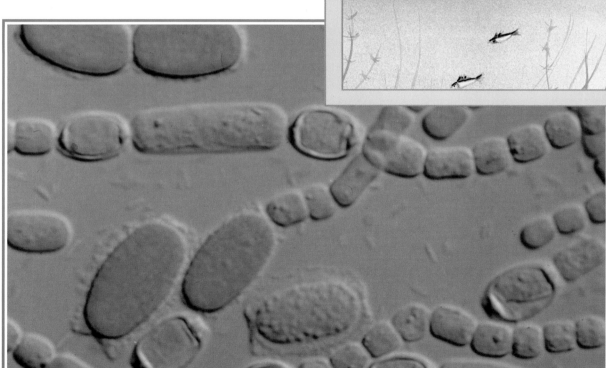

These algae are among the smallest plants in the world. Each of the green shapes is a single cell. Algae like these can only be seen under a microscope.

Tiny moss

Moss is a plant that often grows on walls and trees. Each one of these moss plants is only about $1/2$ inch (1 cm) tall.

Now try this

Look at tiny moss plants using a hand lens.

You will need:
a hand lens, moss plants, paper, a pencil

1. Find some moss on a tree or a stone wall in your garden or school grounds. Do not pick it.

2. Hold the hand lens about 4 inches (10 cm) above the moss.

3. Look through the hand lens. Now try drawing all of the tiny

leaves and flowers that you can see.

Big Buildings

Big buildings are needed wherever lots of people gather together. Any big building must be built carefully, using strong materials. Otherwise, it may fall down.

Tall building

This is the Sears Tower in the city of Chicago. It is the tallest building in the world. Tall buildings have to be very straight. Otherwise they might topple over.

Big stadium

A large building like this **stadium** must be strong, so that it will not collapse under its own weight.

Now try this

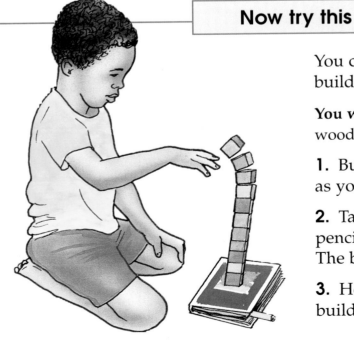

You can see for yourself why tall buildings need to stand straight.

You will need:
wooden blocks, a book, a pencil

1. Build a tower of blocks as tall as you can on top of the book.

2. Take down the tower. Push the pencil into the pages of the book. The book will not be level.

3. How tall a tower can you build now?

Big and Small Bridges

A bridge must be able to carry the weight of whatever goes over it. Small bridges can be simple to build. But big bridges are built by using strong shapes, such as arches.

Simple bridge

A small bridge can be a simple plank of wood. If this bridge were any longer, it would bend in the middle.

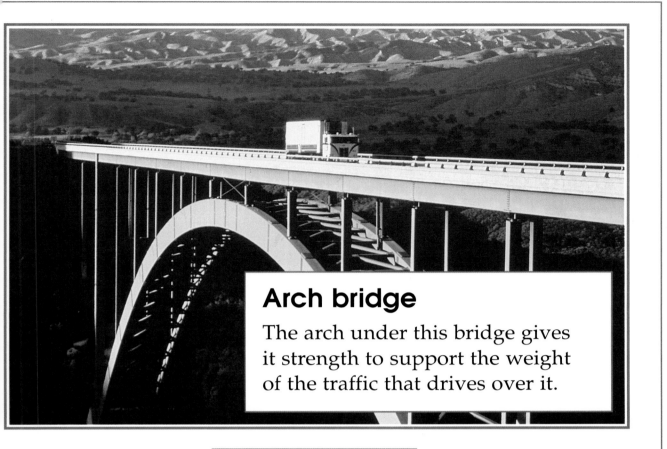

Arch bridge

The arch under this bridge gives it strength to support the weight of the traffic that drives over it.

You can see how strong an arch shape is.

You will need:
two strips of cardboard, each about 12 inches (30 cm) long, some books

1. Make two equal piles of books about 8 inches (20 cm) apart.

2. Place one strip of cardboard over the books, to make a simple bridge. Is this bridge strong or floppy?

3. Now fit the other strip of cardboard between the piles of books, so that it forms an arch.

4. Place the flat cardboard over the arch. Which bridge is stronger?

Biggest and Smallest

Some of the biggest things are **galaxies**. Some of the smallest things are **atoms**. Everything is made up of atoms. They are too small to be seen by the human eye itself.

Big galaxy

The Earth moves around the sun. The sun is one of the stars in a huge group of stars called a galaxy. This picture shows a galaxy called Andromeda.

Did you know?

The biggest bird's eggs in the world are laid by the ostrich. An ostrich egg is usually 7 inches (18 cm) long, three times as long as a chicken's egg.

Smallest parts

This picture shows two types of atoms. The color has been added to the picture by a computer.

Now try this

You can see how atoms arrange themselves in a **solid**, like salt.

You will need:
marbles, modeling clay, a hand lens, table salt

1. Look closely at a few grains of salt, using the hand lens.

2. You should see that most of the grains are box-shaped. This shape is called a **cube**.

3. See if you can join the marbles together to form a cube, using the modeling clay. This is how atoms join together to make a grain of salt.

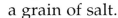

Glossary

algae A tiny plant found in water

aspirator An instrument used to collect and study insects

atoms Tiny parts from which everything is made

bacteria Very small living things that only have one cell

callipers Instruments used to measure sizes or distances

cells Small parts that make up plants and animals

comparing Looking at the differences and similarities between two or more items

cube A solid shape with six square sides

cubit A measurement of distance, first used by the Ancient Egyptians

galaxies Huge groups of stars in space

microchip A small part of an electronic device

microscope An instrument that is used to examine objects more closely

model A small copy of an object

nutrients Substances contained in food that are important for health and growth

planet A solid body in space that travels around a star. The Earth is a planet.

solid A substance that has a definite shape and size

stadium A large building used for athletics

suspension bridges Bridges that are held up with cables attached to towers

Index